THE JADE STONE

A Chinese Folktale

adapted by Caryn Yacowitz

illustrated by Ju-Hong Chen

Holiday House/New York

Second Adviser Third Adviser First Adviser Emperor Imperial Ambassador Empress Imperial Guard Horse Master

Pekinese

Library of Congress Cataloging-in-Publication Data
Yacowitz, Caryn. The jade stone / adapted by Caryn Yacowitz: illustrated by Ju-Hong Chen—1st ed. p. cm.
Summary: When the Great Emperor of All China commands him to carve a Dragon of Wind and Fire
in a piece of perfect jade, Chan Lo discovers the stone wants to be something else.
ISBN 0-8234-0919-8
[1. Folklore—China.] I. Chen, Ju-Hong, ill. II. Title. PZ8.1Y23Jad 1992 91-17934 CIP AC [E]

To my mother and father
C.Y.
To my dear daughter, Mi-Le
J.C.

Jade Sculpture   Chan Lo,   Apprentice   Spectators   Congratulator   Announcer   Chair Carrier   Band
The Stone Carver

Long ago in China there lived a stone carver named Chan Lo. Chan Lo spent his days carving birds and deer and water buffalo from the colored stones he found near the river.

"How do you know what to carve?" his young apprentice asked.

"I always listen to the stone," replied Chan Lo. "The stone tells me what it wants to be."

People came from near and far to buy Chan Lo's carvings.

So it happened that when the Great Emperor of All China was given a perfect piece of green-and-white jade stone, one of the advisers in the Celestial Palace thought of Chan Lo.

The humble stone carver was brought before the Great Emperor of All China.

Chan Lo bowed deeply.

"I want you to carve a dragon," the emperor commanded, "a dragon of wind and fire."

"I will do my best to please you," Chan Lo said.

The emperor's men carried the precious stone to Chan Lo's garden.

Chan Lo had never seen such a perfect piece of jade. The green-and-white of the stone was like moss-entangled-in-snow.

The great emperor had commanded "a dragon of wind and fire." Chan Lo wondered if that was what the stone wanted to be.

He spoke to the stone:

"Here I stand, O Noble Stone, to carve a creature of your own. Whisper signs and sounds from rock that I, your servant, may unlock."

Chan Lo bent down and put his ear to the stone. From deep inside came a gentle sound. "Pah-tah," it went. "Pah-tah, pah-*tah*."

"Do dragons make that sound?" Chan Lo wondered.

Perhaps the dragon's tail splashing in the ocean says "Pah-tah, pah-*tah*," he thought. But he was not sure.

That evening Chan Lo ate his rice cakes and sipped his tea. He thought about dragons.

In his dreams he heard "Pah-tah, pah-*tah*."

The next morning Chan Lo went to the garden. The stone was spring-water-green in the morning light.

Chan Lo said:

"Here I stand, O Noble Stone, to carve a creature of your own. Whisper signs and sounds from rock that I, your servant, may unlock."

Chan Lo put his ear to the green-and-white jade and listened. Softly, the sounds came. "Bub—bubb—bubble," he heard. "Bub—bubb—bubble."

"Do dragons make that sound?" Chan Lo asked himself. "Perhaps a dragon rising from the wild waves blows bubbles through his nostrils."

But these were not mighty dragon bubbles coming from the rock. They were gentle, lazy, playful sounds.

Chan Lo's heart grew heavy, for he had not heard the emperor's dragon.

That evening, when Chan Lo ate his rice cakes and sipped his tea, he tried again to think about dragons.

But when he went to bed, he heard the sound of "Bub—bubb—bubble" in his dreams.

In the middle of the night, Chan Lo awoke. He walked into the moonlit garden. The stone shone silvery-green in the moonlight.

He would listen one last time.

"Here I stand, O Noble Stone,
to carve a creature of your own.
Whisper signs and sounds from rock
that I, your servant, may unlock."

He put his ear to the stone.
Silence.
Chan Lo ran his hands over the jade. His fingers felt tiny ridges. "S-s-s-ah, S-s-s-s-s-ah, S-s-s-s-s-s-s-ah," went his fingers over the stone.
Do dragons have ridges?

"Yes," he decided, "they have scales. Scales on their tails and bodies. And their scales might say 'S-s-s-ah, S-s-s-s-ah, S-s-s-s-s-s-ah,' if one dared to touch them."

But Chan Lo knew these small, delicate ridges were NOT dragon scales.

Chan Lo could not carve what he did not hear, but he was afraid to disobey the emperor. His fear weighed heavy in him like a great stone as he picked up his tools and began to carve.

He worked slowly and carefully for a year and a day.

Finally, the carving was complete. Early in the morning, before the birds were awake, Chan Lo and his apprentice wrapped the jade carving in a cloth and set out for the Celestial Palace.

Chan Lo entered the Great Hall where the three advisers sat waiting for the Great Emperor of All China.

He placed the jade stone on the table in the center of the room.

Soon the emperor's advisers grew curious. They scurried to the jade stone and peeked under the cloth.

"No dragon," whispered the first, softly.

"NO DRAGON!" exclaimed the second.

"NO DRAGON!" shouted the third.

At that moment, the emperor himself was carried into the Great Hall.

"Show me my dragon of wind and fire!" the emperor ordered.

The advisers whisked the cloth away.

"This is not my dragon," the emperor roared, his eyes dark with anger, his voice rolling like black thunder.

"PUNISH HIM! PUNISH HIM!

PUNISH HIM!" the three advisers chanted.

"Oh mighty emperor, there is no dragon of wind and fire," Chan Lo said, his knees shaking like ginkgo leaves in the wind. "I did not hear it. I heard these three carp fish swimming playfully in the reeds in the pool of the Celestial Palace."

"HEAR IT? You did not HEAR it!" The emperor's words burned Chan Lo's ears. "TAKE HIM AWAY!"

Chan Lo was lifted by two palace guards, then dragged down many flights of stairs and thrown into a black prison cell.

The emperor ordered that the jade stone be removed from the Celestial Palace. The carving was placed outside, near the reeds of the reflecting pool.

The advisers gathered around the emperor.

"Chop off his head," said the first.

"Boil him in oil," said the second.

"Cut him into a thousand pieces," said the third.

But the emperor was so angry, he could not decide which punishment to choose.

"I will let my dreams decide," he said.

That night, the emperor dreamed of fish playfully slapping their tails in green water. "Pah-tah, pah-*tah*."

In the morning the emperor's advisers asked, "What punishment have you chosen?"

"My dreams have not yet decided," said the emperor.

The next night the emperor dreamed of fish gliding smoothly through deep, clear water. "Bub–bubb–bubble, bub–bubb–bubble."

In the morning the emperor's advisers again asked him, "What punishment have your dreams chosen?"

"My dreams have still not decided," said the emperor.

On the third night, the emperor groaned and tossed in his sleep, but he did not dream. He awoke in the darkest hour of the night. A strange sound filled the room. "S-s-s-ah, S-s-s-s-s-ah, S-s-s-s-s-s-s-ah."

The emperor got out of bed and went toward the sound. He hurried down the corridors, through the Great Hall, and out into the moonlit garden. There, by the reflecting pool, was the jade stone. Next to it stood the stone carver's apprentice, running his fingers down the scales of the three carp fish. "S-s-s-ah, S-s-s-s-s-ah, S-s-s-s-s-s-s-ah."

The shining scales of the jade carp glowed in the moonlight. The fishes' slippery bodies were reflected in the pool. They seemed ready to flick their tails and swim among the reeds.

The emperor sat near the pool, gazing at the jade stone until his advisers found him at sunrise.

"What punishment have your dreams chosen?" they asked.
The great emperor smiled an imperial smile.
"Bring Chan Lo before me," he said.

Chan Lo bowed deeply before the Great Emperor of All China, ready to receive his terrible punishment.

"You have disobeyed me, Chan Lo, but you are a brave man to defy the Great Emperor of All China," said the emperor. "You have carved the creatures that were in the stone. I, too, have heard them. These three carp fish are dearer to me than any dragon of wind and fire. What reward would you have?"

Chan Lo bowed lower still. "Great Emperor, your happiness with my work is my reward. I wish only to return to my village and carve what I hear."

"You will carve what you hear," said the emperor, "and return to your village in a way befitting the Master Carver to the Great Emperor of All China!"

Pah-*tah*!

In 1917, the merchant A.L. Gump was in Beijing, China, buying jade for his San Francisco store, when a Mandarin told him a story about a jade carver and an emperor. Years later, Mr. Gump's son Richard described the story in his book, *Jade, Stone of Heaven*. When I heard the story, I could not forget it. I decided to expand it into a picture book for children. Like Chan Lo's sculpture, it took a year and a day (or maybe a little longer).

Caryn Yacowitz

The art for each picture consists of an ink and watercolor painting prepared on handmade rice paper. I tried to evoke the look of ancient hand-colored oriental wood-block prints.

Ju-Hong Chen